W9-BRR-848

The Sesame Street
BEDTIME STORYBOOK

Featuring Jim Henson's Muppets

Written by

Tony Geiss

Emily Perl Kingsley

David Korr

Jeffrey Moss

Robert Oksner

Patricia Thackray

Illustrated by

Tom Cooke

A. Delaney

Joseph Mathieu

Marc Nadel

RANDOM HOUSE · CHILDREN'S TELEVISION WORKSHOP

Copyright © 1978 Children's Television Workshop. MUPPET Characters © 1971, 1972, 1973, 1974, 1978 Muppets, Inc. All rights reserved under International and Pan-American Copyright Conventions.
® Sesame Street and the Sesame Street sign are trademarks and service marks of the Children's Television Workshop. Published in the United States by Random House, Inc., New York, and simultaneously in Canada by Random House of Canada Limited, Toronto, in conjunction with the Children's Television Workshop. Library of Congress Cataloging in Publication Data: Main entry under title: The Sesame street bedtime storybook. SUMMARY: A collection of twelve read-aloud stories featuring the Sesame Street Muppets. 1. Children's stories, American. [1. Short stories] I. Geiss, Tony. II. Cooke, Tom. III. Children's Television Workshop. PZ5.S47 [E] 77-93774 ISBN 0-394-83843-2 ISBN 0-394-93843-7 lib. bdg. Manufactured in the United States of America.
67890

CONTENTS

Grover, Messenger of Love

Grover was skipping happily down the lane, strumming his lute, when he heard the sound of someone crying. It was a beautiful princess weeping by her garden wall.

"Do not cry, beautiful princess. I, Grover, will play you a happy tune on my cute little lute," he said.

"It won't help," she wailed. "I am crying because of this stupid wall."

"But it looks like such a nice wall—all covered with beautiful vines," said Grover.

"It is a horrible wall. I am the lovely Lucretia. My one and only love and next-door neighbor, Lorenzo, lives on the other side of that wall. We used to laugh and play together all the time. But one day my father's pet goat, Lulu, ate up Lorenzo's father's long red woolly underwear that was hanging on the line to dry."

"What a sad story," said Grover, beginning to sniffle.

"Wait. It gets sadder," said Lucretia. "Lorenzo's father was so angry, he built this awful wall so Lulu would never darken his clothesline again. And from that day to this, Lorenzo and I have been apart."

4

Joe Mathieu

"Boo, hoo, hoo," wailed Grover. "May I borrow your hanky, please?"

"Wait a minute. It gets even sadder," said Lucretia. "I wrote this love letter for Lorenzo and sprinkled it with my best perfume. But he will never read it."

"Why not?" asked Grover. "You mean he cannot read yet?"

"Oh, he can read. But I can't get the letter to him because of this stupid wall."

"Say no more, fair princess. I, Grover, will be your Messenger of Love." Grover took the letter, doffed his feathered cap, and bowed *very* low. Just then, Lulu the goat charged up behind Grover and butted him high into the air.

"Air-mail special-delivery love letter!" yelled Grover as he flew o-o-over the wall.

He landed smack on top of the handsome Lorenzo. "*Oof!* Where did you come from?" cried Lorenzo as he crawled out from under Grover.

"From the other side of your father's wall. I have a love letter from the fair Lucretia," said Grover.

Lorenzo eagerly read the letter and swooned from happiness and too much perfume.

"Good fellow, please take this to the lovely Lucretia," said Lorenzo,

5

handing Grover an enormous chest full of precious jewels.

"This is very heavy," gasped Grover, sitting down on one end of a seesaw. "How will I ever get it over the wall?"

The handsome Lorenzo, who was also quite bright, had an idea! He stood on a chair and shouted to Grover, "Get ready, furry Messenger of Love!"

Then Lorenzo jumped onto the end of the seesaw, and Grover was hurled into the air.

"Here I go again," cried Grover, as he flew over the wall.

"Oh, Messenger of Love, do you bring a message from Lorenzo?"

"I do have a little something for you," croaked Grover.

"Wow! Jewels!" exclaimed the fair Lucretia. "Just what I needed." Then she reached behind a nearby rosebush and pulled out a framed, life-sized oil portrait of herself.

"You must take this to my love," she said.

"I am going over the wall *again*? Being a Messenger of Love is a lot of hard work!" said Grover, collapsing into Lucretia's velvet swing. "Please excuse me a minute," he said. "I must take a little nap."

"This is no time for a rest," said Lucretia. She gave the swing a great big push, and once again Grover went flying. As he landed at Lorenzo's feet, his head crashed through the portrait.

"It is I, Grover, in a beautiful portrait of your love," he said, smiling bravely up at Lorenzo.

"Here, Grover. While you were away I baked Lucretia's favorite treat—Tickleberry Tarts." Lorenzo gave Grover a huge silver tray piled high with steaming tarts and helped him up on a trampoline. "Hurry, Grover, before they get cold."

"One...twoooo...threeeee!..." sang Grover. "Here comes your tired, furry Messenger of Love," he said as he zoomed o-o-over the wall, and landed in Lucretia's goldfish pond.

"The tarts!" cried Grover. "I must save them." Grover balanced the enormous tray on his cute little tummy

and backstroked madly to shore.

"Oh, joy. My favorite treat— Tickleberry Tarts!" exclaimed Lucretia as she took the slightly soggy tarts from Grover. "Grover, you must take another gift to Lorenzo for me. I have just the thing."

"Back to Lorenzo!" wailed Grover. "Oh! Oh! I am so-o-o *cold* and so-o-o *tired*. But I, Grover, Messenger of Love, cannot disappoint such adorable lovers."

"Look!" said Lucretia. "A suit of armor. Lorenzo will look so romantic in it."

"Maybe you could just blow him a little kiss instead?" asked Grover hopefully.

"Don't be silly, Grover," said Lucretia, stuffing him into the armor.

"*Ouch!* It pinches," yelped Grover from inside the armor. "Lucretia, this is so-o-o heavy. How can I get over the wall?"

"Love will always find a way,"

9

Lucretia said sweetly. "Come along now. Hop upon my golden skateboard and I'll give you a shove right down that little hill."

WHOOOOSH! As Grover whizzed down the little hill, he could hear Lucretia calling, "Remember to jump, Grover!"

Speeding faster and faster, Grover saw the wall looming before him. Then…CLANG!! The visor on his helmet slammed shut. In the darkness Grover could hear Lucretia yelling, "Jump! Jump!! Jump!!!"

But it was too late.

C R A S H ! ! ! !

Grover smashed *through* the wall.

The two lovers found themselves staring at each other through a Grover-shaped hole in the wall. Together again, they embraced.

"Lucretia!"

10

"Lorenzo!"

"Oh, Mom-mee!" came a muffled cry from Grover.

He was all tangled up in a pair of long red woollies that had been hanging out to dry. The Messenger of Love staggered over to Lucretia and Lorenzo, trailing the long red woollies behind him.

"Thank you for bringing us together once again, noble sir," chimed Lorenzo and Lucretia.

"Oh, it was nothing," wheezed Grover. "Now that you are happy once more, it is time for me to bid you farewell and go home to my mommy and my nap."

"Wait! One last favor," begged Lucretia. "On your way home could you please deliver these party invitations to our hundreds of friends and relations? We're having a party to celebrate!"

"EEEEEEEYYYYYYYYIIIIIIII!" screamed Grover as he fell over backward in a faint.

The King and the Fireman

Once upon a time, in a palace in a faraway kingdom, there lived a king. Now the king and everybody in his kingdom were living quite happily until one day an awful thing happened. The king's palace caught on fire.

"Oh, my!" yelled the king. "My palace is on fire. Fireman, fireman! Come quick!"

The fireman heard the king
yelling and quickly ran to the
rescue.

"Here I am, Your Majesty!" cried
the fireman. "Ready with my trusty
hose!"

He had arrived just in the nick of
time, and he put out the fire. Well,
the king was so grateful that he
immediately issued a royal
proclamation:

"I hereby proclaim that from now

13

on, everyone in my kingdom will quit his or her job and become a fireman!"

So all of the king's subjects quit their jobs and became firemen. Well, it wasn't very long before the king began to have problems. In fact, the very next morning the king was playing with his royal blocks, and he hurt his finger.

"Oh, no!" cried the king. "I've cut my royal finger! Quick, somebody call the Royal Doctor!"

The Royal Doctor was summoned to the king's side. But she didn't *look* like a doctor. She was wearing a fireman's suit.

"I'd like to help you," she said. "I *used* to be a doctor, but I fight fires now. Maybe if I blew my siren your finger would feel better." And she pushed the siren button on her fire

truck. "I hope that helps," she said, and left.

"Boy-oh-boy!" cried the king. "I hurt my royal finger and there's no one to fix it. Only people blowing sirens, so that now my ears hurt, too!"

Well, if that wasn't bad enough, the next day the king was waiting for his mail, and he had another problem.

"Where is my royal mail?" asked the king. "I am expecting a very important royal letter. Where is the Royal Postman? Send for the Royal Postman immediately!"

So the Royal Postman was sent for, but...he arrived wearing a fireman's uniform.

"I'm not a postman any more," he told the king. "I'd love to help you, but you ordered everyone to be a fireman. So I'm a fireman now."

"But who's going to deliver my mail?" wailed the king.

"I don't know. But...here's a hose. See you around." And he left.

The king was very upset. "I can't read a fire hose!" he grumbled. "I sure wish I had some royal mail to read."

Well, if that wasn't enough, it wasn't long before the king had yet another problem.

14

"Wow, am I hungry!" said the king. "I'm in the mood for a royal baloney sandwich. Where is the Royal Cook? Royal Cook, bring me my lunch!"

So the Royal Cook was summoned. But when he appeared, he too was dressed as a fireman.

"I used to be the Royal Cook," he said, "but I'm a fireman now, because that's what you ordered."

"But I'm hungry!" yelled the king. "I want a baloney sandwich!"

"I'm sorry," said the cook. "Try eating this." And he handed the king his fireman's hat. "Maybe with a little ketchup it won't taste too bad," he said. And he left.

"Boy-oh-boy-oh-boy!" complained the king. "What kind of a kingdom is this? I'm hungry, but there's no one around but firemen who give me hats to eat. I have a feeling that something's wrong around here."

Well, the king sat and thought, and he realized that he had made a big mistake. So he made a new proclamation:

"I hereby proclaim that everybody should go back to his or her old job, and from now on only firemen should be firemen, and everyone else should

just do his or her own thing!"

And the doctor, the postman, the cook, and everybody else immediately took off their fireman suits and started celebrating.

"Now that I'm a doctor again, I can fix your finger!" exclaimed the doctor.

"And now I can deliver the royal mail right away!" cried the postman.

"And here's that royal baloney sandwich you wanted," said the Royal Cook.

And so the king had learned a very important lesson. It takes all kinds of people to make a world, and if everybody had the same job, it would be pretty hard to get things done. It would be pretty silly, too.

Oscar Has a Bad Dream

One night Oscar the Grouch had a bad dream. In fact, he had a terrible dream.

Oscar dreamed that one morning he opened the lid of his old, banged-up trash can and it wasn't old and banged-up any more. In fact, it was all shiny and pretty and freshly painted and tied with a big red bow. Oscar was so surprised that all he could do was open his mouth, but no noise came out. He looked again at the nice white paint and the flowers painted on the outside, and opened his mouth again. Only this time, a lot of noise came out.

"I don't believe it. I just don't believe it! Somebody ruined my nice dirty, dented-up garbage can. This is awful. Look how yucchy it looks now. I am so upset I'm going to Mr.

Hooper's store and have a nice, cold anchovy ice-cream soda to cool me off."

Oscar went into Mr. Hooper's store, climbed up on the stool and said, "Hi, Mr. Hooper. I'm rotten and I hope you're the same. Give me my old favorite, an anchovy ice-cream soda. And don't expect me to say please, because grouches don't say nice things like that."

Mr. Hooper smiled at Oscar and said, "Anchovy soda? I'm sorry, but we don't have any anchovy ice cream. We only have nice-tasting ice cream, like vanilla and chocolate and strawberry."

"Wait a minute. Are you telling me that you don't have any of my favorite ice cream any more? No more spinach ice cream? No more onion ice cream? Just disgusting vanilla and chocolate? Well, never mind.

"The Mudman is coming with my weekly delivery of delicious mud. I'll just wait for him."

Oscar went back to his trash can, hiding his eyes so he couldn't see how nice it looked, and went inside. Soon there was a knock on the lid. Oscar opened it and stuck his head out. It was the Mudman.

"Boy, am I glad to see you. I can hardly wait for my nice, delicious bottles of mud."

"Mud? Excuse me, Oscar. But I'm not bringing you any mud. I'm bringing you some nice, fresh bottles of milk!"

"Milk?? Are you kidding? I don't drink milk. It's too good for you. I want my slimy old mud. That's what I want."

"But, Oscar, I wouldn't bring anybody *mud* to drink. That's

17

disgusting. Oh, by the way, your garbage can looks very nice."

"Ughhh!" cried Oscar. "I don't believe this is happening to me. No anchovy ice cream. No mud. My poor, wonderful, beat-up garbage can all shiny and ruined. I know what I'm gonna do. I'm gonna see my old friend Leon at the crummy dump. He'll be in his nice, broken-down shack with rags for curtains and he'll make me feel better. Yep. That's where I'm going because I can't stand it here."

Oscar began walking to the dump. He walked in the gutter, of course, because that was his favorite place to walk. Usually Oscar found old tin cans or empty soda bottles to kick, and all sorts of trash and rubbish to pick up and save.

"Hey. Wait a minute. What is going on?? I've been walking for five minutes and there's no trash in this gutter. It is clean. In fact, everything looks neat and clean. This is terrible! Boy, wait until I see my friend Leon at the dump. Something weird is going on around here."

In his dream, Oscar arrived at the dump. And he was surprised again.

"I must be seeing things!" Oscar cried. "Leon, my old grouchy friend, is all neat and dressed up! The old town dump, which used to be messy and dirty and full of busted furniture and trash, is now all neat and clean and the trash isn't trash any more. It's fixed up and looks nice and new again! And Leon's house is fixed up and has new white curtains. This is terrible. This is yucchy! This is disgusting! Leon, what is going on??"

"Why, Oscar, I don't know what you're talking about. I wouldn't like an awful, messy, dirty dump. And I wouldn't live in a broken-down, falling-apart old shack with dirty rags for curtains. But come inside and have a nice hot plate of delicious chicken stew."

"Delicious chicken stew?? You used to make delicious garbage stew from potato peelings and eggshells with an old galosh tossed in for flavor. Chicken stew? *Yucchy!*"

Oscar didn't know what to do. His trash can was covered with flowers and fresh paint. Mr. Hooper didn't have anchovy sodas or Oscar's favorite ice cream. The Mudman had milk instead of nice, gooey mud. The gutters all over town were nice and clean. Even the town dump was all fixed up and spiffy.

"I must be going crazy," cried Oscar. "There's no trash blowing around here. Everything's so neat and clean I can't stand it! How's a grouch supposed to live in a place like this?"

Oscar's terrible dream made him toss and roll around in his sleep. Finally, he fell right out of bed and onto the floor and woke up. "Hey! I was only having a bad dream.

Whew! I was getting worried. Heh, heh! Boy, wouldn't it be terrible if everything really was all nice and neat? Thank goodness that was only a bad dream. Guess I'll go outside now and see who I can yell at."

Oscar pushed up the lid of his garbage can and almost fell out. His garbage can looked just the way it did in his dream! It was freshly painted, it had flowers all over it, and tied around it was a big red ribbon. Oscar looked around wildly. There was no trash in the gutter. The street, sidewalk and gutter were clean.

"Oh, no. I'm wide awake and it looks like I'm still dreaming! What is happening to me??"

"Why, nothing's happening to you, Oscar," Maria said to him.

"Everything is nice and clean because we're having Clean-Up Week here on Sesame Street."

"Whew!" said Oscar. "For a minute I thought I was dreaming again. Clean-Up Week, huh? Well, I'm so happy that it's not my dream coming true that I might even help."

So Oscar straightened the bow on his garbage can and went back inside.

"But don't tell anybody!" he yelled as the lid slammed shut.

19

Grover and the
Twenty-Six Scoops

It was Grover's first day as an
ice-cream scooper at Ye Olde ABC
Ice-Cream Parlor. He stood proudly
behind the counter, his brightly
polished scoop in hand, ready to help
his first customers. In came Betty
Lou and her little brother, Herbie.

"Greetings, little girl and little
boy," said Grover, peering up over
the counter. "Welcome to Ye Olde

ABC Ice-Cream Parlor. The Special
of the Week is . . ."

"Please, sir," said Betty Lou. "I
already know what I want—a double-
dip Vanilla cone, no sprinkles. What
do you want?" she asked Herbie.

"Well . . . ummmm . . . errrr . . .
geeee . . . I don't know," said Herbie.
"What flavors do you have?"

"We have twenty-six terrific

flavors," said Grover. "One for each letter of the alphabet, and I know them all by heart. At Scoop School we had to recite them every morning after breakfast."

"Twenty-six flavors!" said Herbie. "Oh, boy, I want to hear them all."

"Oh, no," groaned Betty Lou. "Herbie, you know you can never make up your mind."

"I want to hear every flavor," said Herbie.

"Certainly," said Grover. "You are the customer, and the customer is always right. Are you ready? Here we go!"

"Wait, mister," said Herbie. "I can't see into the ice-cream bins."

"You are right, little boy," said Grover. "I will show you each delicious flavor."

Grover whipped out a cone and scooped out the first flavor as he proudly called its name. "Starting with the letter A we have Anchovy Applesauce.... Next, B—Baloney Bonbon, C—Cactus Crunch, D—Dinosaur Dip, E—Eggplant Eclair, F—Fruitcake Fiesta Flip," sang Grover, scooping one brightly colored flavor on top of another. "G—Gumball Goop, H—Honey Hamburger Hash, I—for Imitation Igloo..." Grover stopped a minute to catch his breath.

"What's next?" asked Herbie excitedly.

"Next?" said Grover. "Next we have this sweet little flavor that begins with J—Jiffy Jellybean Jive. And then we have K for Kangaroo Kringle, and here's the bin for L—L for Lavender Licorice."

"Can you wait a minute, mister?" asked Herbie. "I can't keep up with all the flavors."

"I am sorry, little Herbie," said Grover. "I cannot stop or I will lose my place in the alphabet. Then I will have to start all over again from the beginning."

21

"From the beginning!" groaned Betty Lou. "We'll never get to V for Vanilla. . . ."

"Let me see now. I will try to continue," said Grover. "We are up to the letter M for Mushroom Mango Mash—*my* special favorite. For N we have Nifty Noodle Nectar. O is for Orange Oyster Oops!, P—Pickle Parfait, Q—Quacky Quip. (Is that not a ducky flavor?) R—Ravioli Ripple."

The stack of scoops got higher and higher. Herbie's and Betty Lou's eyes got bigger and bigger as they watched the leaning tower of scoops.

"Oh, my gosh. It's going to fall!" said Betty Lou.

"Do not worry. I, Grover, will not let these scoops fall down." He swayed back and forth, barely balancing the tipsy tower of ice cream.

"Hey, Betty Lou," whispered Herbie. "This is better than the circus."

"Phew," said Grover, as he steadied the scoops. "That was a very close call. Thank goodness I was tops in balancing at Scoop School. Now, Herbie, do you see anything here that you like? I do not want to rush you, but this cone is getting very difficult to balance—even for Grover."

"I haven't seen all the flavors yet," said Herbie.

"Oh, that is right," said Grover. "I nearly forgot. Now, what letter was I up to?"

"You were up to S, mister," said Betty Lou.

"S!" said Grover. "Scrumptious S for Sardine Swirl." Then he dipped into the ice-cream bin marked T—for Triple Turkey Trifle. "And now we have U—for Upside-down Uglifruit. . . . And now, V—V for Vanilla. . . ."

"That's it! That's the one!" cried Betty Lou, jumping up and down

with joy. "I'll have a Vanilla cone, please."

"Oh! Oh! I am so sorry, little girl," said Grover. "But I cannot stop until I get to the end of the alphabet."

Grover dashed over to the bin marked W. He quickly scooped out Watermelon Wobble.

"Now on to the X flavor... XXXXXXX. That stands for many kisses. (You would *love* this flavor!) It is even better than Y for Yak Yogurt Yum-Yum.

"Oh, my goodness," said Grover. "Only one more flavor to go. I think I can do it." Grover dipped his furry little arm into the last bin at the far, far end of the counter. He brought out the Z scoop—Zucchini Zip. The twenty-sixth and last scoop!

"Oh! Oh! I am so-o-o-o-o pooped," wheezed poor Grover as he staggered around under the dripping tower of scoops. "They never told me it would be like this back in Scoop School. Herbie, please— tell me which flavor you want. One scoop or two? Plain or with sprinkles?"

"Well... ummmm... errrr... geeee..." said Herbie.

Herbie! Make up your mind," wailed Betty Lou. "You've seen every flavor in the place, and I want my Vanilla!"

"Herbie thought about it and thought about it. He thought for a *long* time. Finally, he looked up at Grover and said, "Wellll... ummmm... maybe if you started all over from the beginning..."

"WHAT?" shrieked Grover. "All over again from the beginning!!!"

Grover threw up his hands, launching the enormous cone straight up in the air. Ice cream flew in all directions.

"He's going bananas!" said Betty Lou.

"Gee, mister," said Herbie. "Don't get so upset. I'll take Vanilla, too!"

"EEEEEEEYYYYYYYIIIIIII!" screamed Grover, and he fainted away right into the Anchovy Applesauce– Baloney Bonbon–Cactus Crunch– Dinosaur Dip–Eggplant Eclair– Fruitcake Fiesta Flip–Gumball Goop– Honey Hamburger Hash– Imitation Igloo–Jiffy Jellybean Jive– Kangaroo Kringle–Lavender Licorice– Mushroom Mango Mash– Nifty Noodle Nectar– Orange Oyster Oops!–Pickle Parfait– Quacky Quip–Ravioli Ripple– Sardine Swirl–Triple Turkey Trifle– Upside-down Uglifruit–Vanilla– Watermelon Wobble–XXXXXXX– Yak Yogurt Yum Yum–Zucchini Zip!

Silly Annabelle

Once upon a time, in a village in a faraway land, there lived a little girl named Annabelle. Annabelle liked to lie in the grass and watch the clouds, and she liked to work in her vegetable garden. She also liked to read books about trains (although she had never seen one because her village was too small to have a train station). But most of all she liked to sing. She would sing all day long, whatever she was doing. Wherever she went people would say, "There goes that Silly Annabelle, singing as always. Do you think she'll ever stop?" But of course she never did.

Then, one day, the people in Annabelle's village woke up to find that a huge yellow dragon, with a tail as long as all Sesame Street, had appeared during the night. He was running around having a wonderful time knocking over fences and chasing cows and digging holes in the street and trampling through the gardens and eating the straw roofs right off the houses and, well ...just making a terrible mess of everything. You can imagine all the trouble a dragon like that would cause.

24

The people in Annabelle's village wondered what to do. Then one old, old man remembered that his great-great grandmother had told him the recipe for a magic powder that would turn big dragons into little dragons.

The people ran to get the things they needed to make the magic powder. They got mushrooms and turnip seeds, a baby's shoe, two blue buttons, a feather from a swan, and the dust from the northwest corner of the attic of the tallest house in the village. They ground everything up together to make the powder. Then the old, old man remembered that you were supposed to put the powder on the end of the dragon's nose.

"Uh-oh," everybody said. "How are we ever going to put the magic powder on the end of the dragon's nose?"

The schoolteacher had an idea. "I'll climb up this tree," he said, "and

throw the powder down, right onto the dragon's nose." But that didn't work. The dragon wrapped his tail around the tree and shook it so hard that the schoolteacher fell out with a loud crash and had to be carried home.

The woman who owned the cheese shop thought they should sprinkle the powder on some cabbages and put them where the dragon would find them and eat them. That way he would get the powder all over his nose himself. But it turned out that the dragon didn't like cabbages and wouldn't go near them.

At last, after a hundred other ideas had failed, Annabelle asked to try. "Oh, Silly Annabelle," everyone said, "how could *you* put the powder on the dragon's nose?"

"I could sing to him," Annabelle answered. "That might work."

Of course, everyone laughed and said, "Silly Annabelle," but in the end they let her try because they didn't know what else to do.

So, feeling very frightened, Annabelle took some of the magic powder in her hand, walked slowly toward the dragon, and began singing. She just made up the words as she went along, and this is what she sang:

Oh, what does a dreaming dragon dream of?
What passes through a dreaming dragon's head?
Does a dreaming dragon dream of toys and candy,
Or of digging holes and eating roofs instead?

Oh, what dreams will make a dragon happy?
What kind of dreams will make a dragon smile?
Do you dream of telling jokes and being friendly,
Or of scaring cows and chasing them a mile?

Oh, what does a dreaming dragon dream of?
Please tell me what I've always longed to know.
Sleep and dream of all the things that dragons dream of.
Won't you dream a dream before you have to go?*

26

*"What Does a Dreaming Dragon Dream Of?" Copyright 1977, David Korr.

The dragon stopped frisking around and pulling up bushes with his tail and began to listen. He started swinging his head slowly back and forth to the song. Then his eyelids began to droop. He got sleepier and sleepier, and at last he stretched out full length on the ground, rolled over on his side, and began to snore. Annabelle bravely tiptoed forward and put the magic powder right on the end of the sleeping dragon's nose.

At first, nothing happened. Then, all of a sudden, the dragon began to shrink. He got smaller . . . and smaller . . . and smaller.

Finally, he was no bigger than a big dog—and since that was just the right size for a pet, Annabelle took the dragon home with her and put

him in her backyard. There he liked to run and play and eat the lima beans Annabelle fed him from her garden. Most of all, though, he liked to listen to her sing.

The people in the village were very proud of Annabelle, and very grateful to her for putting the magic powder on the dragon's nose. They knew now that she wasn't silly at all, and they never called her "Silly Annabelle" again.

Betty Lou Lends a Hand

"My, what a blustery, blowy day," said Bert as he stepped out onto Sesame Street. "This is the strongest wind we've had around here in a long time."

Bert held his coat tightly closed against the wind and noticed that all of his friends were out playing touch football in the yard.

"Hey, everybody," called Bert, holding up a small white envelope in his hand. "Come here! I have something to show you!"

Bert's friends stopped their game of touch football and came over to Bert.

"What is it?" asked Ernie.

"Yeah, what've you got there that's so wonderful?" asked Roosevelt Franklin.

"I bet it's a new paper clip for his paper clip collection," Farley whispered to Grover.

"... Or some new pictures of pigeons or something boring like that."

"Oh, it's so fantastic," said Bert, "I can't wait to show you!"

"So let's see it!" said Prairie Dawn. "We interrupted our game of touch football to come over here and see what it is."

Just as Bert was about to open the envelope and show everybody what was in it, a big gust of wind whipped the envelope out of his hand and blew it up into the air.

"Oh, no!" cried Bert. "My

a lot of friends here. I'm sure someone will be able to get the envelope out of there for you."

"Sure, Bert," said Herry. "I'm the *strongest* person here so I'm sure I can get your envelope back for you. And even if there is only a silly, dumb picture of a pigeon inside, I'll help you get it back.

"Now stand back, everybody, and make way for the *strongest* one of all. I will just lift that fence up into

envelope!! The wind is blowing it away! Help!"

The wind carried the envelope high in the air, twisting and turning it, dipping and darting it, sailing it over a big wooden construction fence and onto the ground on the other side.

"Oh, gosh," wailed Bert. "My envelope's behind that big fence. Now what am I going to do?!"

"Gee, Bert," said Ernie. "You have

the air so you can go underneath and grab your envelope. I bet you're glad *I* am here today! Ya!"

Herry grabbed a corner of the fence and pulled up with all his might, but the fence was very firmly planted and he couldn't lift it out of the ground.

"Gee, Herry, thanks a lot," said Bert. "You are very strong, but it looks like strength isn't what we need to get my envelope back."

"Let me try," said Big Bird. "I'm the *biggest*. I'll just reach right over the top of the fence and get your envelope for you. Even if it is just a silly old picture of a pigeon, it's important to you, so I'll help you get it back. Now everybody watch closely as the biggest one here gets the envelope. Here goes. . . ."

Big Bird stood up on tippy-toes and reached as far as he could over the top of the wooden fence, but the fence was too high. Big Bird couldn't reach far enough to get the envelope.

"I'm sorry, Bert," said Big Bird. "I guess bigness is not what you need, either."

"What you need is *smartness*," said Sherlock Hemlock, "and I am the world's smartest detective. I will get that envelope out of there."

"Ahhh," said Bert. "Smartness. Now that's a good idea."

Sherlock Hemlock went over to a skinny little crack in the fence and put his mouth up against it.

"Now, little white envelope on the ground in there, I, Sherlock Hemlock, the world's smartest detective, am talking to you," he said through the crack. "I think you ought to realize how upset you have made our friend Bert by flying over that fence. And even though you probably have nothing but a silly, boring old picture of a pigeon inside you, I think that the *sensible* thing would be for you to come out of there and stop causing Bert so much distress. Now, what do you say?"

Naturally, the envelope just lay there on the ground. Sherlock

Hemlock threw up his hands. "This silly envelope is *not* responding to logic and reason. I do not understand it."

Bert sighed. "I guess it has no respect for smartness."

"May *I* help?" asked the Count.

"Sure," said Bert. "What do *you* think?"

"I think that you have had three suggestions that did not work. *Three*! You had the strongest, the biggest, and the smartest. That makes three no-good suggestions! Ah-hahahahaha! Happy to be able to help, Bert."

"That didn't help!" snapped Bert.

"Say, Bert," said the Cookie Monster. "Me the *hungriest*. How about this? Me eat this fence up. Then you can go get envelope. Me not do that for silly, boring picture of pigeon. Me do that because me so hungry and fence look pretty good."

"Oh, Cookie Monster," moaned Bert. "I'm ready to try anything. Eating a fence sounds crazy to me, but if you feel up to it . . ."

Cookie Monster went over to the fence and took a great big, huge bite out of it.

"Blecchhh!" he cried. "That the most terrible fence me ever eat! Boy! Need salt! Need ketchup! Need Worcestershire sauce! No way me can eat whole fence that taste like that! Sorry, Bert. Me want to help but there a limit even to what *me* can eat!"

"*Four* terrible, awful, silly, no-good ideas!" yelled the Count.

"How about *me*?" called Rodeo Rosie. "I'm the *loudest*! You just give

31

me a crack at it and I'll have your silly old pigeon picture back in two shakes!"

"Go ahead, Rodeo Rosie," shrugged Bert.

Rodeo Rosie sauntered up to the fence and put her hands up to her mouth.

"NOW LISTEN HERE, ENVELOPE! YOU GIT ON OUTA THERE RIGHT PRONTO, Y'HEAR? I GIVE YA A COUNT OF THREE TO JIST SKEDADDLE RIGHT ON OUT HERE WHERE YA B'LONG!! A-ONE, A-TWO, A-THREE!!" she hollered.

"That certainly was loud," said Bert, rubbing his ears. "But the envelope's still sitting there, just like before. Thanks, Rodeo Rosie, but I guess loudness wasn't what we needed either."

Bert gave a deep sigh. "Say, how about *you*, Betty Lou?" he said. "You're the only one who hasn't made a suggestion. Don't you have

any ideas about how to get my envelope back?"

"Me?" said Betty Lou. "Well, I am not the biggest or the strongest or the loudest or the smartest. All I am is the *smallest*. What could I possibly do for you?"

"I don't know," said Bert. "But the biggest and the strongest and the loudest and the smartest haven't

done much good. I thought you could come up with something."

"Well, let me look," said Betty Lou.

She walked up to the skinny little crack in the fence and looked through. There was the white envelope, still lying on the ground. Betty Lou was about to turn away when she thought of something.

"Hey," she said. "I'm so small that if I held my hand all flat like this . . . and held my arm out straight like this . . . maybe, just maybe I could just squeeze my little arm right through that crack . . . like this . . . and reach your envelope with my fingers . . . like THIS!!"

And she grabbed the envelope with her fingers and pulled it through the narrow crack in the fence. She held it up high for all to see.

"Hooray for Betty Lou!" everyone shouted.

"Wow," she said. "I did it! I didn't have to be the biggest or the strongest or the smartest or the loudest or anything!! In fact, being the *smallest* was just what you needed! How about that!"

"That's right, Betty Lou," said Bert. "Thank you!"

Bert smiled broadly. "Well, now

that we have the envelope back, wouldn't you all like to see what's in it?"

"Oh, we know what it is, Bert," said Ernie. "Just some silly, boring old picture of a pigeon for your scrapbook. We knew that all along. Probably just a silly old pigeon eating birdseed. . . ."

"Or a pigeon walking on the ground," said Prairie Dawn.

"Or a pigeon sitting on a statue," suggested Herry.

"*I'd* like to see what's in the envelope, Bert," said Betty Lou. "Please?"

"Well, as a matter of fact," said Bert, "it just happens to be . . . tickets to the circus for me . . . and all my friends!"

"Tickets? For the circus? For your friends?" said Ernie, swallowing hard.

"For *all* your friends?" asked Big Bird. "Even the ones who kept teasing you about having a dumb old pigeon picture in there?"

"ALL my friends," shouted Bert, happily. "My strong friends . . . and my big friends . . . and my smart friends . . . and my little friends . . . and my fast friends . . . and my slow friends . . . for *all* my friends!"

"Yaaaay Bert!" cried all his friends.

And they all started out for the circus together.

"And on our way to the circus," said Bert, "I'll tell you all about the great pigeon act we're going to see there. This circus has the *best* trained pigeons! We'll actually see a pigeon stand on one foot. And then we'll see a pigeon who *sits down*. And after that, a pigeon eating a piece of bread. . . . And guess what comes after that?! . . ."

Cookie Monster
Has a Bad Dream

One night Cookie Monster had a bad dream. In fact, he had a terrible dream.

In his dream, Cookie Monster went into Mr. Hooper's store and asked for his usual box of cookies. "Cookies?" said Mr. Hooper. "What are cookies?"

"What you mean, 'What are cookies?'" cried Cookie Monster. "Cookies are cookies, my favorite food. Now, gimme cookies!"

"I'm sorry, Cookie Monster. But I don't have any cookies anywhere in the store. And what's more, I don't even know what you are talking about when you ask for cookies. I never heard of cookies."

Cookie Monster couldn't believe his ears. How could Mr. Hooper never have heard of cookies? And how could Mr. Hooper not have any cookies in his store?

"Oh, well. Must be something

wrong with Mr. Hooper today. He never heard of cookies. Me go to different store. They have cookies."

Cookie Monster went into a big supermarket. "Oh, boy, this store have everything. This store going to have cookies, too, me sure."

Cookie Monster walked up and down and up and down, all over the store. He found bread and crackers and doughnuts, but he didn't find any cookies. He went to the manager of the store and said, "Me not find cookies anywhere in this great big store. Where cookies, please?"

"Cookies?" the manager asked. "We don't have anything called cookies. In fact, I've never heard of cookies. What are cookies, anyway?"

"Me not believe this," Cookie Monster said. He went outside and sat down on the curb to think. "Something crazy here. Mr. Hooper's store not have cookies. This great big supermarket not have cookies. And they both say they never heard of cookies. What going on?"

Cookie Monster, of course, was dreaming. In his dream, he sat on the curb and almost started to cry. "What me going to do? Got to find cookies. Me know. Me will go to place where they make cookies. Me will go to bakery. Bakery got to have cookies."

Cookie Monster found a nice bakery and went inside.

"Oh ho, smell that? This place bakery, all right. And look at all those pies and cakes and jelly rolls and loaves of bread and ... where the cookies? Me will ask. Umm, excuse me. Where your cookies?"

"Cookies?" the baker said. "Cookies? I've heard of pies and sweet rolls and cakes and jelly rolls and bread, but I've never heard of cookies."

"Oh, no. Me can't believe this! Nobody has cookies. Nobody even heard of cookies. What me going to do?? Me so hungry!"

Cookie Monster sat down on the curb again. "NO COOKIES? Oh, this most terrible thing that ever happened to me. Me got to think."

Cookie Monster thought and thought. None of the stores had cookies. Even the bakery didn't have cookies. Suddenly, Cookie Monster jumped up.

"Oh, me have great idea. Nobody here ever heard of cookies except me, right?? Well, then me going to *invent* the cookie! Me bake tremendous cookie and then everyone will see what cookie is and what cookie taste like. Me going to bake cookie myself!"

Cookie Monster went back to the supermarket and bought five bags of flour and one big bag of sugar and four pounds of butter and a whole bar of baking chocolate.

Then Cookie Monster went back to the bakery and asked the baker if he could use his kitchen to bake a huge cookie.

"Sure, you can use my kitchen. I've never heard of a cookie, but if cookies taste good, then I'll start baking them myself. Go ahead and use my mixing machine and my work table and my biggest oven. I'd like to see what this cookie thing is and what it tastes like."

Cookie Monster poured the flour and the butter and the sugar and the chocolate into the big mixing machine. The machine mixed them all up together into a huge ball of dough.

"Oh, this smell good already. This going to be greatest cookie me ever tasted."

Then Cookie Monster took the ball of dough and shaped it into one huge, gigantic chocolate cookie.

"Oh, this going to be greatest invention people here ever saw. Me inventing the cookie. Now, everything ready to bake for cookie!"

The baker helped Cookie Monster slide the enormous cookie into his biggest oven.

"Hmm. That cookie thing sure smells good, Cookie Monster."

"It going to taste good, too, Mr. Baker. Cookie is greatest thing you can bake. Better than pie or cake or anything."

Finally the cookie was ready to be taken out of the oven.

"Wow. That thing certainly is big," the baker said.

"That not thing. That cookie. See how good it look? How good it smell? Well, best part is how good it taste. And me can't wait any longer. Me going to taste it right now!"

Just as Cookie Monster was dreaming about taking a big bite of his cookie, Grover woke him up.

"Oh, Cookie Monster, you must have been having a bad dream! You were groaning and tossing around. So I, your pal Grover, woke you up!"

"Oh, Grover. What a terrible dream! Me dreamed that there were no cookies in the whole wide world."

"That is certainly a horrible dream, Cookie Monster," Grover agreed.

"You want to know worst part of dream, Grover? Worst part was waking up and not getting to eat gigantic cookie me baked!

"Me going back to sleep right now."

Who Stole the Count's Thunder?

The thing that the Count loved second-most—right after counting— was his thunder. Every time he counted something—whether it was bats, hats, or cats—lightning would flash and thunder would go BOOM! And he would laugh with joy.

Wherever the Count went, his own special thundercloud went with him. The cloud floated over his head and was always ready to flash and go "BOOM!"—whether it was night or day.

It boomed in the morning, when he counted sunbeams at sunrise.

It boomed at noon, when he counted people eating lunch at Mr. Hooper's store.

And at night in his castle, it boomed when he counted bats to help him fall asleep.

One morning the Count got up, opened the window, and took three deep breaths. "One, two, three beautiful breaths!" he counted. But there was *no thunder*!

Then he brushed his teeth and counted *them*—both of them—and there was no thunder!

40

The Count could not believe his pointed ears! He ran back to the window and looked up.

"Gadzooks!" he cried. "My cloud is gone. *Someone has stolen my thunder!*

"I will ask my friends on Sesame Street if they have seen my cloud," said the Count, and he ran out of his castle.

There was Mr. Hooper counting newspapers in front of his store. "One, two, three," said Mr. Hooper. "BOOM!" went the cloud, and lightning flashed. Mr. Hooper ran into his store.

"There you are, my cloud, my darling!" cried the Count, and he ran down Sesame Street, his cape flying behind him. But just as he got to Mr. Hooper's Store, the cloud sailed away. "Stop, thunder!" cried the Count. But the faster he ran, the faster the cloud floated away. Then it stopped and hung right over Big Bird, who was playing jacks.

"One, two, three jacks," counted Big Bird. "BOOM!" went the cloud. "Sounds like rain," said Big Bird. He opened his umbrella and kept on counting, "four, five, six."

The Count ran toward Big Bird, but the cloud sailed off again—and stopped right over a trash can where

Oscar the Grouch was counting his old shoe collection. "One scruffy old sneaker, two rotten old sneakers ... heh, heh, heh!" "BOOM!" went the cloud ... and it *disappeared*!

"My thunder is gone again!" said the Count, and he headed home. "One step, two steps," he counted sadly as he walked back toward his castle—and he began to cry. "One tear, two tears, three tears. And one sob," he counted. But there was no thunder.

When the Count reached the castle of his next-door neighbor, the Amazing Mumford, he decided to pay him a visit. Maybe the magician could help him get his cloud back!

Inside the castle he found Mumford knee-deep in rabbits. "A LA PEANUT-BUTTER SANDWICHES!" said Mumford, reaching in his hat and

pulling out another bunny by the ears. "Seven hundred and twelve rabbits," he counted. "BOOM!" went the thunder.

The Count looked out the window and there, overhead, was his very own cloud!

"So, Mumford," said the Count, "it is *you* who stole my thunder!"

"Yes," said the magician, "it is I, the Amazing Mumford!"

"You are amazing but not amusing," said the Count. "Why did you steal my thunder?"

"Because every night I could hear you counting bats next door," answered Mumford. "BOOM, BOOM, BOOM!" (The walls are so thin in these new castles.) The noise kept me awake. I was so tired I couldn't lift a hare. So I used magic trick

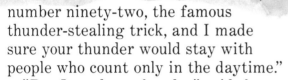

number ninety-two, the famous thunder-stealing trick, and I made sure your thunder would stay with people who count only in the daytime."

"But I *need* my thunder," said the Count. "If I don't count bats, I can't sleep."

"And if you *do* count bats," said Mumford, "*I* can't sleep."

"But I *must* have my thunder," pleaded the Count. "A day without thunder is like a night without wolves! Without my thunder I don't know when I've stopped counting. Without my thunder I don't know when to go 'Ah-haha!' I love my thunder! It makes me laugh. It makes me sing. It clears my sinuses. Besides, it's been in the family for a thousand years. You must get me my cloud back!"

"Wait!" said the Amazing Mumford. "I, the Amazing Mumford, have solved the problem! I will not only give you your cloud, I will give you *two* clouds! A LA PEANUT-BUTTER SANDWICHES!" he cried, and he waved his magic wand.

And—PRESTO!—over the Count's head appeared not one but *two* personal thunderclouds . . . a big noisy cloud for daytime counting, and a small quiet cloud to use at night!

The Count looked up. "One, *two* thunderclouds!" he cried happily. "BOOM!" answered the big cloud. "Ah-haha!" said the Count, getting the last laugh.

And from that day on, the Count had two kinds of thunder—loud thunder for counting in the daytime, and soft thunder for counting at night!

Grover's Bedtime Story

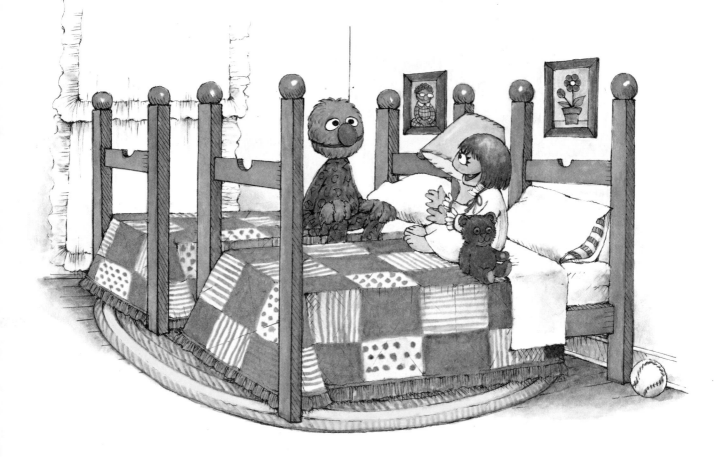

"Thank you very much for inviting me to sleep over at your house, Grover," said Prairie Dawn. "I've had such a good time."

"Oh, it is fun to have somebody come to visit and sleep over," said Grover. "I am glad you could come. But now it is late and I think we had better go to sleep."

"Uh, Grover?" said Prairie Dawn.

"There is just one little thing. I like to hear a bedtime story before I go to sleep. When I am home, my daddy usually tells me a story."

"Hmm. That is a problem," said Grover. "We could call your daddy on the telephone and he could tell you a story over the phone. How would that be?"

"I have a better idea," said Prairie

Dawn. "Why don't *you* tell me a bedtime story?"

"Me?" said Grover. "*Me??* Cute, furry, adorable old Grover? Tell you a bedtime story?"

"Why not?" said Prairie Dawn. "I am sure you know lots of nice stories."

"Er, well," said Grover, "I have not told many bedtime stories before. In fact, *none* is how many bedtime stories I have told. None at all. I really do not know how to tell a bedtime story."

"Oh, I am sure you can do it," said Prairie Dawn. "You just start at the beginning and the rest will take care of itself." She got into bed and pulled the covers up around her chin. "O.K., Grover, I am ready. You can start your bedtime story now."

"Oh, dear," said Grover. "How to do this. . . . Just start at the beginning and see what happens, huh? Ahem. All right. . . .

"Once upon a time . . ." he began. "Yes, that is an excellent *beginning* to my story. Once upon a time! Once upon a time. Once upon a time."

"Uh, Grover," said Prairie Dawn, "what comes next?"

"I beg your pardon?" asked Grover.

"Well," said Prairie Dawn, "all you said was 'Once upon a time.' There has to be more to the story than that! That is just a *beginning* to the story. What happens next?"

"Ohhhh," said Grover. "You want to know what happens next! Of course you do! Heh, heh. Um . . . well . . . let me see. . . .

"Once upon a time," Grover began again, ". . . um . . . well . . . they lived happily ever after! There you are!"

"Grover!" said Prairie Dawn. "What kind of story is that? That is not the way to tell a story! Once upon a time they lived happily ever after? That is ridiculous!"

"You did not like the way it ended?" asked Grover. "I always thought 'they lived happily ever after' was a very nice ending to a story."

"The beginning was O.K., and the ending was O.K. . . . but there was no middle."

"No middle?" said Grover. "What is a *middle*?"

"The middle is the *story* part of the story—where everything happens!" explained Prairie Dawn. "You left out the whole middle part!"

46

"I am sorry, Prairie Dawn," said Grover. "I told you I did not have much experience in telling bedtime stories."

"Well, let me show you how it works," said Prairie Dawn. Then you will know how, and you can tell me *my* bedtime story."

"That is an excellent idea!" said Grover.

"O.K.," said Prairie Dawn. "First you start your story with 'Once upon a time,' just as you did. But then you follow it with the middle part of the story. So here goes:

"Once upon a time there was a king named Roundtree and he had a very smart and beautiful daughter named Victoria Joyce. One day a wicked magician came and put a spell on the three good fairies who were weaving an enchanted cloak in which to wrap the mysterious silver apple so that it could be delivered to the wondrous wizard of the West, so their fingers turned into string beans and they could no longer weave the enchanted cloak. But the brave little girl mesmerized the six fire-breathing dragons that guarded the castle gate and flew on the magic flying horse, Basingstoke, through the skies, dodging the evil eagles and horrid hawks that swooped and darted at her, on to the wizard's palace, where she delivered the silver apple to the wizard all by herself. The wizard was so amazed at Victoria's splendid feats of bravery and courage that he presented her with a beautiful singing bird and a flower that would always be in bloom. The evil witches on the mountains gnashed their

teeth and pulled out their hair
because they had wanted the
singing bird and the amazing ever-
blooming flower but they knew they
could not fight against such a
glorious girl as Victoria Joyce and
Victoria sailed home to her father's
castle on the back of a great golden
swan ... and ... and here is where
you put the ending part on, Grover,
and ... she lived happily ever after!

There. You see how easy it is
to tell a bedtime story? But you
absolutely must have the middle
part or else it is not a story at
all. Do you understand now,
Grover? ... Grover? ... Grover??"

But Grover had fallen fast asleep.

"Oh dear," said Prairie Dawn.
"Now I've *done* it. I told such a good
story that I put Grover to sleep. Now
what am I going to do? I'll be up all
night."

Just then the door opened and
Grover's mommy came into the
room.

"Would you like to hear a bedtime
story, Prairie Dawn?" asked Grover's
mommy. "I used to tell bedtime
stories to Grover but he would
always fall asleep right after the
'Once upon a time' part. He never
heard the middle and the end. It
would be a great treat for me to be
able to tell a bedtime story to
someone who could stay awake long
enough to hear the 'happily ever
after' part."

"Oh, thank you," said Prairie
Dawn. And she curled up under the
covers as Grover's mommy sat down
beside the bed.

"Once upon a time ..." began
Grover's mommy. . . .

49

The Case of the Mysterious Mud Puddle Monster

One day, Big Bird decided to take a walk around Sesame Street. He opened his door and stepped out— right into a mud puddle. "Oh, drat," he said. "Phooey." But it was too nice a day to fret, so he went on his way, forgetting all about the puddle.

Next he stopped at Mr. Hooper's store for a birdseed soda and an apple. Prairie Dawn was minding the store for Mr. Hooper, and Cookie Monster was also there, having a cookie sandwich. Big Bird drank his soda, ate his apple, and chatted for a while with his friends.

First he went to the home of Oscar the Grouch, who lived in a trash can and collected trash. Big Bird wanted to give him some old papers he had saved. Oscar said, "Swell, now leave me alone," and Big Bird left, happy that Oscar liked his present.

Then he remembered that Ernie and Bert had invited him to come see their new tablecloth, so he decided to visit them. After he had admired the tablecloth, which was covered with blue and white squares, he told Ernie and Bert how much he liked it, and set off for home.

51

When he got there, he saw Sherlock Hemlock, the world's greatest detective, looking through a magnifying glass at something on the ground.

"Hi, Mr. Hemlock," said Big Bird. "Are you looking for clues with your magnifying glass?"

"Indeed I am, Big Bird," said Sherlock Hemlock. "I, Sherlock Hemlock, the world's greatest detective, am investigating my newest case."

"Oh, boy!" said Big Bird. "What kind of case is it?"

"It's THE CASE OF THE MYSTERIOUS MUD PUDDLE MONSTER," answered Sherlock Hemlock.

"The Mud Puddle Monster!" said Big Bird, feeling just a little frightened. "What's a Mud Puddle Monster?"

"That," said Sherlock Hemlock, "is the mystery. I don't know what a Mud Puddle Monster is. But I'm going to find out, or I'm not Sherlock Hemlock, the world's greatest detective." Sherlock Hemlock pointed his finger at the ground. "I already have some clues," he said. "Look. These are footprints. And do you see where they start? They start right here, at this mud puddle. That means that whoever made these footprints came *out* of the mud puddle! Now, who else would come out of a mud puddle but a Mud Puddle Monster?"

"My goodness, you're clever, Mr. Hemlock," said Big Bird, bending over to look at the muddy footprints and the puddle. "Hmmm," he said thoughtfully. "That looks just like the mud puddle *I* stepped in a little while ago."

"Egad!" said Sherlock Hemlock. "Another clue. When you stepped in this mud puddle, you made the Mud Puddle Monster *mad*. That is why he came out of the puddle."

"He's mad? Do you mean he's mad at *me*?" asked Big Bird, feeling a little more frightened than before.

"Yes, indeed," said Sherlock Hemlock. "He's mad at you. He's also quite large."

"Oh, dear. How can you tell that?" Big Bird wanted to know.

"From his footprints," Sherlock Hemlock told him. "They're enormous. Only someone very, very big could make footprints like that. Now, let us follow them and see where they lead."

Big Bird and Sherlock Hemlock followed the mysterious footprints, which led straight to Oscar's trash can. Big Bird knocked on the lid, and Oscar peeked out. "What do you want now?" he said.

"We're looking for the Mud Puddle Monster," said Big Bird. "Have you seen him? He's great big, all covered with mud, and he's real mad."

"No, I haven't seen him," said Oscar. "But I'll help you look for him. If he's as nice as he sounds, I'll invite him home for dinner."

Big Bird and Sherlock Hemlock

and Oscar then followed the footprints right down the street and into Mr. Hooper's store. They asked Cookie Monster and Prairie Dawn if they had seen the Mud Puddle Monster.

"He's great big," said Big Bird, "and all covered with mud, and he's real mad, and he probably has lots of teeth and a nose shaped like a doorknob."

Cookie Monster and Prairie Dawn shook their heads. "I've never heard of a Mud Puddle Monster," said Prairie Dawn. "And I know I've never seen one."

"But he came right into the store," Big Bird insisted.

"Well, we not see him," Cookie Monster said.

"Egad," said Sherlock Hemlock. "Another clue. The Mud Puddle Monster came right into the store and no one saw him. That can only mean one thing. The Mud Puddle Monster is invisible!"

"Oh, no!" said Big Bird, feeling more frightened than ever. "He's invisible! Now what do we do?"

Sherlock Hemlock looked at the footprints through his magnifying glass. "We must keep following the footprints," he said. "Come along. They go right back out of the store."

Cookie Monster and Prairie Dawn decided to come, too. Prairie Dawn hung up a sign that said, "Closed. Back soon—I hope." And they all set off together.

The tracks now led to Ernie and Bert's door. Big Bird suddenly realized something. "Hey! That Mud Puddle Monster went everywhere I did. I went to Oscar's can, Mr. Hooper's store, and Ernie and Bert's apartment, too!"

"Of course," said Sherlock Hemlock. "It is all beginning to add up. He was following you."

Big Bird didn't say anything, but he was as frightened as he'd ever been.

Then Sherlock Hemlock said, "Wait. Here's another clue. The Mud Puddle Monster is still inside Ernie and Bert's apartment. See? The footprints go in, but they don't come out!"

Big Bird knocked loudly on the door. Ernie opened it, and Big Bird said, "Ernie, Ernie, a monster is hiding in your apartment!"

"Oh, dear," said Ernie. "What kind of monster?"

"It's the Mud Puddle Monster," said Big Bird. "He's great big and he's mad and he's all covered with mud."

"He has lots of teeth, too," added Prairie Dawn.

"And a nose like a doorknob," chimed in Cookie Monster.

"And ears like tennis shoes," Big Bird went on, getting more excited.

"You can't see him because he's invisible," Sherlock Hemlock reminded everyone.

"I want to invite him home for dinner!" shouted Oscar.

"This is terrible," said Ernie. "What are we going to do?" And with that, they all began talking at once. Soon Bert came to the door to find out what was going on.

Big Bird pointed to the muddy footprints. "Look, Bert," he said. "Those muddy footprints go into your apartment, and they don't come out again."

"Of course they don't come out again," said Bert. "All the mud came off on our carpet. I've just been cleaning it up. Next time you come to visit us, Big Bird, I wish you would wipe your feet."

"Me?" said Big Bird. "Why? What did I do?"

"I just told you," said Bert. "You got mud all over our carpet when you came to see our new tablecloth. Those are *your* footprints."

"*My* footprints?" Big Bird looked down at his feet. Sure enough, his feet and the footprints were the same size and shape.

Sherlock Hemlock also looked at Big Bird's feet. Then he announced, "Aha! The final clue. I have solved the mystery!" He turned to Big Bird and said, "*You* are the Mysterious Mud Puddle Monster."

"Who?" said Big Bird. "Me?"

"Yes," said Sherlock Hemlock. "I, Sherlock Hemlock, the world's greatest detective, have piled clue upon clue, sifted all the evidence, and arrived with astounding swiftness at the conclusion to another baffling mystery. *You* are the Mud Puddle Monster."

"Oh, dear," thought Big Bird. "How silly. *I'm* not the Mud Puddle Monster. Why, there's probably no such thing as a Mud Puddle Monster." But he didn't tell Sherlock Hemlock that. "After all," he said to himself, "even the world's greatest detective makes mistakes."

"Well," said Sherlock Hemlock, "I must be going now. My job here is finished. Don't thank me. It's all in a day's work." Then he waved good-bye to everyone, turned, and went off, looking about him through his magnifying glass for his next case.

"Phooey," said Oscar. "Some Mud Puddle Monster. I'm going home."

"I'm just glad everything is all right after all," said Prairie Dawn. "Now I can go back to minding Mr. Hooper's store."

"Me come with you, Prairie Dawn," said Cookie Monster. "All the excitement make me hungry."

"Boy," said Ernie. "I think I feel like reading a nice un-scary story with no monsters. What do you say, Bert?"

Bert said he thought that was a good idea.

Big Bird, who was very happy to know he wasn't being followed by a big, angry, muddy monster with a nose like a doorknob, decided to take a nap. "Solving mysteries always makes me sleepy," he said.

ZZZ Z Z ZZZZ

The Count Has a Bad Dream

One night the Count had a bad dream. In fact, he had a terrible dream.

In his dream, the Count was outside raking leaves. "Aha," cried the Count. "Look at all these lovely leaves. They are falling down very fast. Of course I will count them all. I will have a wonderful time, because there are *so many* wonderful leaves to count. I can hardly wait. So I will begin.

"One beautiful leaf. Two beautiful leaves. Uh . . . two beautiful leaves. I said that already. Ummm. One, two . . . what *is* this? I can't remember what comes after two. How can I count all these beautiful leaves when I can't even count? There must be some mistake. I, the Count, not able to count? Ridiculous! I will count again.

"One lovely little leaf. Two lovely little leaves. Oh, rats and bats! What comes next? I cannot count! This is the worst possible thing that could happen! The Count has *forgotten how to count*!

"Shhh. Do not tell anyone. But what shall I do? I, the one and only Count, must remember how to count. I will go to my favorite restaurant, the Numeral Diner, and order a bowl of delicious number soup. I will look at all the lovely little numbers in the soup—and then eat them. *That* will help me remember how to count."

The Count put down his rake and went off to the Numeral Diner.

"Hiya, Count. What'll it be today?" the man behind the counter asked. "We've got some French fried 17s on the special."

"Ah, good afternoon. I will have a large bowl of number soup, please. And make sure that it has a lot of numbers, please."

As the Count ate the big bowl of number soup, he was sure that seeing and eating all those numbers would help him remember how to count.

"Ah, that was wonderful. Now I

feel much better. I will go outside and count all the cars.

"Oh, look at all those cars zipping by. I can hardly wait to count them. Here I go. One speeding car. Two speeding cars. Uh . . . ummm . . . two speeding cars. Er . . . cobwebs and candlesticks! I cannot *remember*! The number soup didn't help me remember. This is terrible! This is horrendous! This is also not nice. The Count *must* count again. I know. I will go to the number store and buy a big bag of numbers. That will help me remember how to count.

"I will have two dozen assorted numbers, please," the Count said to the salesperson in the number store. "And do not bother to wrap them. I will use them here."

The Count took all the numbers and played with them. Then he lined them up and looked at them. Finally he said, "Yes, yes. I am sure that seeing all these numbers has made me remember how to count. I am going

right outside and start counting again.

"Yes, yes. Look at all the people walking by. Perfect! I will count all the people. One nice person. Two nice persons. Ah . . . umm. . . . Two nice persons. Oh, no! . . . I have forgotten again. I cannot count any more! What am I going to do?? I know. I will go to the number factory, where they make all the numbers. That will help me remember how to count."

So, in his bad dream, the Count went to the number factory. He went to the number assembly line, where they were putting together millions of numbers. One woman was fitting crosspieces on number 4s. A man was assembling rows of the number 8.

The Count walked up and down the number assembly line, looking at all the big and little numbers as they were being put together.

"Oh, what a wonderful place this is!" cried the Count. "I love the

number factory. I feel so wonderful that I am sure that now I remember how to count. I am going outside right now and start counting again."

The Count left the number factory and saw all the trucks outside, bringing material to make the numbers.

"Trucks! All kinds of trucks. I will count them immediately. I love to count trucks. One terrific truck. Two terrific trucks. Umm. . . . Two terrific trucks. Oh, darkness and dungeons! How could this happen to me, the Count? I must count again. I know. I will go back to school and learn how to count again. What a clever Count I am!"

The Count went into a school and found a class that was learning how to count. He sat down with all the children and listened to them learning how to count. When they went out to play during recess, he stayed in the classroom. He studied the numbers on the blackboard. When the children came back to the classroom, the teacher called on the Count and asked him to stand up and count to ten.

"Oh, counting to ten is so simple," the Count said. "And now that I have studied here in your school, I can count to five thousand and ten. But you asked me to count to ten, so I will do it. I will count ten children! Here I go. One . . . two . . ."

The Count stopped. "But . . . but . . . this is impossible. I cannot count past two! I . . . I must be dreaming."

And, of course, he *was* dreaming.

At just that moment, the Count woke up. He sat up in bed, shaking all over.

"Oh, what a terrible dream. I was dreaming that I forgot how to count. But I must go back to sleep again to find out if I ever remembered how to count. What if I never remember how to count?"

The Count put his head back on the pillow, pulled up the covers, and said, "One sheep, two sheep, three sheep, four sheep, five sheep . . ." and fell asleep.

Good Night, Rubber Duckie

"It's getting late, Ernie," said Bert, "and my whole family of sisters and brothers and aunts and uncles and cousins are coming to visit us first thing in the morning." Bert snuggled down into his warm, cozy bed. "Why don't you finish what you're doing and get into bed?"

"I'm almost finished, Bert, old pal," said Ernie, putting his toothbrush back in the holder. "I washed my face and hands and I brushed my teeth. And now I'm ready to get ready for bed."

"Ready to get ready? What do you mean?" asked Bert.

"Well, I can't jump into bed just like that," replied Ernie. "I have to make sure I have everything I need for sleeping. Now let's see. . . . First let me check and see if I have my blanket and my pillow. . . ."

"Of course you have your blanket and your pillow, Ernie," said Bert. "Your bed has the same blanket and sheets and pillow that it's always had."

"Well, that's true," said Ernie, "but you can't be too careful. I wouldn't want to get into bed and all comfy-cozy and *then* find that my pillow or my blanket wasn't there."

"All right, all right," said Bert. "Your pillow and blanket are there. Now will you *please* go to bed!"

"Just a second, Bert," said Ernie. "I have a few other things to check."

"Oh, brother," sighed Bert.

"Hmm," said Ernie, looking around. "My alarm clock is set to go off in the morning. . . . My night light is on in case I need to get up and go to the bathroom during the night. . . . My hockey stick is ready in case anybody comes and invites me to a midnight game of hockey. . . . And my Rubber Duckie . . . my Rubber Duckie is . . . my . . . OH, NO!"

60

Joe Mathieu

"What's the matter?" asked Bert.

"My Rubber Duckie! My Rubber Duckie's not on my bed!" yelled Ernie.

"Come on, Ernie," said Bert. "Your Rubber Duckie is always right there on your bed. I'm sure it's there."

"No, no, it's not," sobbed Ernie. "How can I possibly go to sleep without my Rubber Duckie?!"

"Millions of people have been doing it for years, Ernie. Come on, go to sleep, and we'll find your Duckie in the morning."

"SLEEP WITHOUT RUBBER

DUCKIE?" yelled Ernie. "What if I told you to go to sleep without your paper clips? Huh? Huh? What then?"

"That's different," said Bert.

"It is not! And I'm not going to sleep without my Rubber Duckie!" said Ernie. "And you're going to help me find him."

"Ohhhhhh no," said Bert. "What *I* am going to do is lie here in my nice, warm, cozy bed and go to sleep. If you want to stay up all night looking for your Rubber Duckie, go ahead. But I'm going to sleep. Good night!"

"All right, Bert," said Ernie. "Whatever you say. I'll find Rubber Duckie all by myself. YOO-HOO! RUBBER DUCKIE! RUBBER DUCKIE, WHERE ARE YOU?"

"All right, all right, I'll help you." Bert gave in. "Come on, let's find your Rubber Duckie so we can both get some sleep."

"O.K.," said Ernie. "You look in the refrigerator, and I'll look in the coat closet."

"In the refrigerator?" said Bert. "What would your Rubber Duckie be doing in the refrigerator?"

"You know how hungry he gets just before he goes to bed," said Ernie.

Bert looked in the refrigerator. There were pickles and salamis and leftover meat loaf and grapefruits and applesauce and Ernie's ice skates— but no Rubber Duckie.

Ernie checked the coat closet. There were hats and coats and jackets and galoshes and gloves and his old stuffed toy elephant—but no Rubber Duckie.

"I'm looking in the bathroom," shouted Bert. He found towels and soap and toothpaste and toilet paper and a shower curtain and a

washcloth and Ernie's cowboy hat—
but no Rubber Duckie.

"I'll check out the toybox,"
suggested Ernie. "Maybe he fell in
there after we played with our toys
tonight." Ernie found his fire engine
and his blocks and his paint set and
his Messy Bessy doll and his racing
cars and his marking pen and his
dollhouse and his dinosaur model kit
and a piece of pepperoni pizza—but
no Rubber Duckie.

"I'm checking under the beds,"
said Bert. He looked under the beds
and found some shoes and slippers
and a book and a baseball and
Ernie's R collection and Ernie's
ukelele and a package of marigold

seeds—but no Rubber Duckie.

"I'll check the laundry hamper.
Maybe he fell in there while I was
getting undressed," said Ernie.
Ernie looked in the laundry hamper
and he found socks and undershirts
and pants and sweaters and pajamas
and underpants and his fishing rod
and his basketball—but no Rubber
Duckie.

"I give up," said Ernie, exhausted.
"I've looked everywhere. I'm just
going to have to try to sleep without
Rubber Duckie. I don't know how,
but I'll try."

"That's the spirit," said Bert. "I'm
sure we'll find Rubber Duckie in the
morning."

"I certainly hope so," said Ernie, crawling sadly into bed. He pulled up the covers and put his head down on the pillow with a sigh. Just then there was a great, big, loud SQUEAK!

"Rubber Duckie!" cried Ernie. "You were there all the time, under my pillow. Oh, Rubber Duckie! I'm so happy to find you!"

"*Now* will you go to sleep, Ernie?" asked Bert.

"Sure, Bert," said Ernie. "What in the world are you doing up so late? Don't you remember? Your whole family of brothers and sisters and aunts and uncles and cousins are coming to visit us first thing in the morning! We don't want to be all tired and baggy-eyed! Why don't you go to sleep? Good night, Bert. And good night, Rubber Duckie."

64